Honey

David Ezra Stein

SCHOLASTIC INC.

To bees.

ISBN 978-1-338-57153-0

Copyright © 2018 by David Ezra Stein. All rights reserved. Published by Scholastic Inc., 557 Broadway, New York, NY 10012, by arrangement with Nancy Paulsen Books, an imprint of Penguin Young Readers Group, a division of Penguin Random House LLC. SCHOLASTIC and associated logos are trademarks and/or registered trademarks of Scholastic Inc.

The publisher does not have any control over and does not assume any responsibility for author or third-party websites or their content.

12 11 10 9 8 7 6 5 4 3 2 1   19 20 21 22 23 24

Printed in the U.S.A.   40

First Scholastic printing, March 2019

Design by Eileen Savage

Text set in Green Std

The art was created using bamboo pen, watercolor, and a hint of white acrylic.

It was his second year.
"I'm back!" he said.

His stomach growled like another bear.

As he dug and scraped for things to eat,
he remembered honey.

Warm, golden, sweet,

clear, slowly flowing,

spicy, aromatic,

sparkling with sunlight—

"Honey!"

But it was too soon for honey.

He tried to forget.

But the warm grass smelled as sweet as—

And the sap seemed as sticky as—

And the meadow as gold as, and the stream
as clear as, and the berries bursting like—

"Honey!"

But it was too soon for honey.

The days turned hot and still.

Clouds cracked and grumbled in a heavy sky.

With a rush came the rain.

He had forgotten how good
a rain could be.

It splattered on his head
and shivered down his back.

And after, it was hot and still again.

But still not time for honey.

"Ouch!"

(Busy bees don't like to be bothered.)

He soaked his muzzle in the water.

It was good and cool.

He lay back and watched
the fat clouds trundle by.

Then he found a waterfall, and
was very busy for a long time.

One day he heard a buzz,
and in a flash, he ran.

It was time for honey!

Warm, golden, sweet, clear, slowly flowing, spicy, aromatic, sparkling with sunlight—

"Honey!" Just as good as he'd remembered.

He lapped it up, and licked
his paws for a long time.

The nights cooled

and the days grew crisp.

A sleepy bear sat and
remembered the summer,

and thought how good it had been.